Soccer Battle

by Margo Sorenson

Perfection Learning®

Cover & Inside Illustrations: Sue Cornelison
Designer: Emily J. Greazel

To Jim, Jill, Jane, and Brendan for being the
best family team ever!

About the Author

Margo Sorenson was born in Washington, D.C. She
spent the first seven years of her life in Europe, living
where there were few children her age. She found books to
be her best friends and read constantly. Ms. Sorenson
wrote her own stories too.

Ms. Sorenson finished her school years in California,
graduating from the University of California at Los
Angeles. She taught high school and middle school and
raised a family of two daughters. Ms. Sorenson is now a
full-time writer, writing primarily for young people.

After having lived in Hawaii, Minnesota, and
California, Ms. Sorenson now lives in California with her
husband. When she isn't writing, she enjoys reading,
sports, and traveling.

For information, contact
Perfection Learning® Corporation
1000 North Second Avenue, P.O. Box 500
Logan, Iowa 51546-0500.
Phone: 1-800-831-4190
Fax: 1-800-543-2745
perfectionlearning.com

Paperback ISBN 0-7891-5879-5
Cover Craft® ISBN 0-7569-1108-7
3 4 5 6 7 PP 10 09 08 07 06

Contents

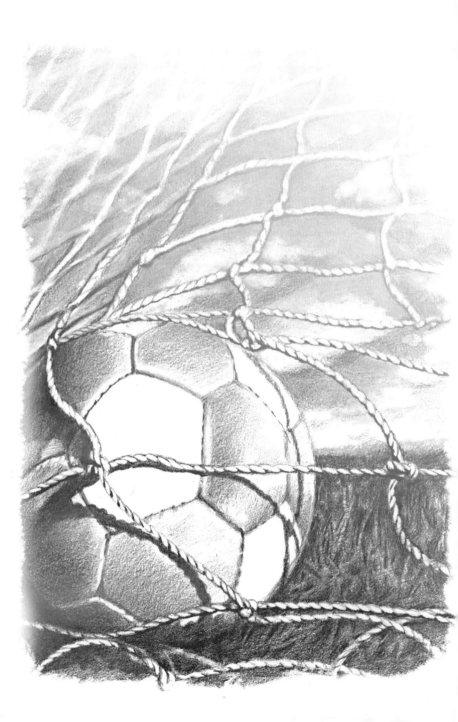

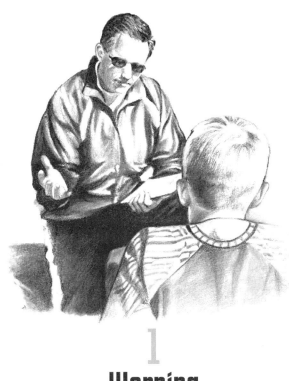

1

Warning

"Jared! I'm open!" a voice yelled across the soccer field.

Jared raced across the grass. He knocked the soccer ball ahead of him. Yeah, Marcus was open. But he wanted to take the shot on goal himself. So what if it was only a practice with his teammates? He had a reputation to keep up.

All around him, he could hear his friends shouting in the crisp fall air.

"Go, Jared!"

"See Marcus!"

"Hey, skins! Mark up!"

"Go wide, Jared!"

"Go, shirts! Go!"

Suddenly, Chas, one of the skins defenders, barreled toward him.

No way, buddy, Jared thought. He tapped the ball forward. Then he faked to the right. He left Chas stumbling onto the grass. Jared grinned.

He streaked toward the corner of the penalty box, plunging past two more defenders. At the 18-yard line, he was in the clear.

"Shot!" someone yelled.

Jared settled the ball with the inside of his foot. Then he took aim.

BOOM! He sent a long, hard shot to the far post.

The ball spiraled through the air. It arced toward the corner of the net.

Yes! Jared told himself. His heart began to lift.

SMACK!

Jared watched in disbelief as the ball hit the crossbar and shot back toward the field.

His teammates groaned.

"No!" he shouted.

TWEEEET!

"All right, Thunder," Coach Mulvey called out from the sideline. "That's enough short-field scrimmage practice for today." He gestured with his clipboard. "Come on in. We'll do some drills next. But I want to talk with you first."

Jared jogged slowly to the sidelines. He wiped his sweaty face with his shirtsleeve. He dropped down on the grass next to Marcus.

The other half of his "skins" team joined him. They picked up their shirts off the grass and put them back on.

"Hard luck on the goal," Marcus said. He wiped his forehead with his shirttail.

"Yeah," Jared said. He shrugged. "That's the way it goes." He reached out to grab his water jug. He drank thirstily. Then he screwed the top back on.

That *was* the way it had been going lately, Jared repeated silently. He had been missing too many shots in the last few games. Why? Scoring had always been so easy.

"Well, Thunder," Coach Mulvey was saying to the guys on the grass. "We have some work to do. We have to win all our games. Remember, the Sting is still undefeated. We play them again a week from Thursday. And they're the only team that's beaten us so far."

"We'd better beat them this time," Marcus whispered to Jared. "We have to get to the play-offs."

"We will," Jared said in a low voice. Inside, he winced. He'd better get his scoring back. The Olympic Development Program scout would be at the play-offs. That could be his chance!

"We have to increase our shots on goal. And our accuracy," Coach said. He looked at Jared.

Why was Coach looking at *him*? Jared asked himself. He frowned. Other guys hardly ever even *took* a shot on goal. They *never* scored. Why pick on him? He still had the league record for scoring, didn't he?

"We have to beat the Sting, so we can get to the play-offs. Then we can win the league too. Don't forget about the San Diego tournament on Veteran's Day weekend."

Jared straightened his shoulders. He looked at Coach.

"Some of the best teams in Southern California will be there. We'll need to score. So let's do a shots-on-goal drill," Coach Mulvey said. "One-on-one."

Jared held back a sigh. Shooting drills never really helped him that much. Being able to score had always been different for him.

Somehow, making shots had always been easy. It was like the magnet experiment in eighth-grade science class. The net almost pulled the ball right into it whenever he took a shot.

Until the last few games, he admitted to himself. He yanked some grass blades out of the turf and tossed them aside.

"You know the drill," Coach directed. "Ramon, you'll be keeper. Chas, you start out as the server at the 18. The rest of you divide up. Challenge, take it down, and score. Let's go!"

Jared pulled himself up off the grass. He glanced at Marcus. "Shooting drill," he grumbled.

Marcus shrugged. "Guess we could all use it," he said. He got up and turned to join a group at the half line.

Jared bit back the words he wanted to say. He jogged next to Marcus toward the half line.

When it was his turn, Jared waited for the whistle. He crouched slightly, weight on the balls of his feet. Ten yards away, Ivan grinned over at him.

"Bet I score!" Ivan challenged.

"Uh-huh," Jared mocked. "You wish."

TWEEEET! Coach Mulvey's whistle shrilled across the field.

Jared took off downfield. He watched Chas boot the ball toward them. Ivan sprang forward.

Jared closed in on the ball. Using his shoulder, he pushed Ivan off the ball. Jared collected the ball with his instep. Then, dribbling fast, he zigzagged toward the sideline.

He sensed Ivan putting on a burst of speed. No chance! Jared told himself.

He bolted toward the corner of the six-yard box. His flashing feet booted the ball ahead of him.

Behind him, he heard Ivan's breath coming in ragged bursts.

Now! Jared commanded himself. He twisted around out of Ivan's path. Settling the ball, he swung his foot back. Then he chipped the ball high into the air toward the far post. Let the net be the magnet, he begged silently.

Shouts filled the air. Ivan ran past him and skidded to a stop. His shoulders were slumped in defeat.

"Go!" Marcus's voice rang out.

"In there!" another player shouted.

Make it! Make it! Jared urged silently, watching the ball.

The ball swooshed through the air—and skimmed past the left goalpost. It bounced through the grass behind the end line. No goal.

Jared stared at the ball bouncing away. Again? he asked himself.

Ramon shook his head and jogged to retrieve it.

The field was silent. Jared clenched his fists. Another miss. Right in front of everyone.

"Next!" Coach Mulvey shouted. Ramon flicked the ball to Chas with his instep.

TWEEEET! The drill began again. Marcus and Armando ran out for the pass.

Jared jogged slowly to the back of his line.

"Hard luck," Kenneth said, turning to face him.

"Yeah," Jared said. He shrugged.

"You can score. You'll get it back," Kenneth said.

Jared only grunted in reply.

Get it back, he grumbled silently. What made everyone think he'd lost it? He stubbed the toe of his shoe into the grass.

Twenty minutes later, Coach Mulvey blew the last whistle.

Jared and his teammates straggled off the field. They flopped on the grass in front of Coach. Jared unlaced his cleats and peeled his socks down. Then he ripped his shin guards off, tossing them in a heap.

Next to him, Marcus stripped off his shin guards too. He slid his feet into his sport slip-ons.

"Tough practice," Marcus said under his breath.

"Yeah," Jared agreed. He frowned and unzipped his soccer bag. Carelessly, he stuffed his shoes, socks, and shin guards inside.

"Listen up," Coach barked out. He thumped his clipboard for emphasis. "We're playing the Invaders this Thursday. They're not in the running for the league play-offs. But we still need to beat them to *get* to the play-offs. Remember, the Sting is undefeated."

Jared shut his eyes for a moment. Coach said there'd be an ODP scout watching at the play-offs. Jared's heart leaped as he thought about the Olympic Development Program.

Jared hoped that someday he could play pro soccer. The ODP could be the first step. Besides, playing ODP soccer could help him get a college scholarship. That would get Mom and Dad off his case. He sure wouldn't get to college on his grades. Jared tightened his mouth. He had to be in that play-off game and make the ODP.

"We need to focus on taking shots," Coach was saying. "Remember, percentages say that for every seven shots on goal you take, one has the chance of scoring. So be sure you practice on your own. That's defenders too," Coach warned.

Was Coach looking at him again? Jared wondered. Back off, he wanted to snap at him.

"One more thing," Coach added. "We're getting a new player. He'll be at practice Wednesday. He's a striker from San Carlos who got a waiver to play for us. His name is José Ramirez."

Jared snapped to attention. A new striker? This José guy had better not take *his* position.

"See you at practice Wednesday," Coach finished.

Everyone got up off the grass. Jared grabbed his soccer bag and walked next to Marcus.

They climbed the steps to the parking lot. Cars waited with their headlights on. A few bikes were chained to a fence.

"See you at school tomorrow," Marcus said, unchaining his bike.

"At prison, you mean," Jared joked. "I can't believe how much work old Mr. Wilson is giving us in social studies."

"Uh-huh," Marcus agreed. "Like we don't have anything else to do." He wheeled his bike out of the rack.

"Gotta go. There's my dad," Jared said, spying the old blue Pontiac. He saw another face through the car window. "Oh, great. My ugly sister is with him."

Marcus laughed. "She's not ugly. She's hot," he said. "Besides, she's your twin. So if she's ugly, then you must be too."

"Stuff it," Jared teased back. He punched Marcus lightly on the arm. "Don't get hit by the crosstown bus on your way home. We need you at striker," he said.

"Yeah, right," Marcus retorted, grinning. He rode off into the night.

"How was practice?" Dad asked when Jared opened the car door.

"Okay," Jared mumbled. He flung his soccer bag on the floor.

"Translated, that means he didn't score enough," JoDee taunted from the front seat. She turned around and made a face at him.

"Put a sock in it!" Jared retorted. "I guess *you* score on every shot you take. Oh, that's right, *you* don't take any shots since you're a goalkeeper."

"At least *I* practice," JoDee sneered. "I don't think I'm Mr. Magic on the soccer field. Gotta look cool, right? Can't act like it's too important. And definitely can't be bothered with practicing!" She narrowed her eyes at him.

"JoDee! Jared!" Dad snapped. "Knock it off."

Jared leaned back against the seat, his jaw set. JoDee was so annoying. He'd rather shut up than argue with her.

Joad the Toad, as he called her, always did everything perfectly. She was a "Little Miss Follow-the-Rules." It was enough to drive him crazy.

"Jared just bugs me, Dad," JoDee complained. "He's too much 'the man.' "

"Let me handle it, JoDee," Dad said. He steered the car out of the lot.

Jared watched the apartment houses slide past the car window. He would just have to be sure he made his shots count. And who was this José guy? What was that going to do to his chances to make the ODP as the best striker on the Thunder?

This José person had better not mess up his plan.

14

2

Challenge

Tuesday morning, Jared dropped into his desk in social studies. The tardy bell rang for sixth period. He'd just made it.

"Actually made it on time today, eh, Mr. Crowley?" Mr. Wilson asked from the front of the room. Old Wilson tried to act tough, but he just couldn't cut it, Jared thought.

"Uh-huh," Jared mumbled, shoving his backpack under his desk. He turned to Marcus sitting next to him and rolled his eyes.

"It's a good thing," Mr. Wilson said. "I was just about to give out the new social studies assignment."

Yippee! Jared wanted to say, but he bit back the words. He was already in enough trouble in this class. And he had to bring up his grade. If he didn't, he'd be in even bigger trouble. He wouldn't be going to San Diego for the November tournament. His parents had made that very clear.

He slumped down in his seat.

"Before we begin, I want everyone to greet our new student," Mr. Wilson announced.

The rustling of papers and books stopped. Everyone looked around. Jared looked too.

"This is José Ramirez," Mr. Wilson said. He gestured to a new face in the back row.

Jared blinked. José? That was the name of the new player on the Thunder. The guy was in his social studies class too?

José's face turned as red as his shirt collar. He stared down at his desk.

Jared saw Maribel and Helene lean their heads together and whisper. They glanced over at José and giggled. Jared wanted to snort.

"Take out your assignment notebooks, class," Mr. Wilson was saying. "Get ready to write down the assignment."

Jared sighed and began doodling on his notebook. He could remember this junk without writing it all down. Looking around the class, he saw students flipping pages and getting ready to write. This had better be an easy assignment. He didn't want to have to work too hard to get his grade up.

"You will be giving an oral report on Greece," Mr. Wilson began. "You will each choose one aspect of Greek culture as your topic."

All right! Jared told himself. If there was anything he could do, it was talk. This would be easy. He'd be able to bring up his grade with no problem.

Mr. Wilson was writing on the whiteboard with a purple marker. "Copy this down," he was saying.

Jared frowned. Fine. He wrote the word *Greece* on his paper.

"Ancient Greece was a beautiful civilization," Mr. Wilson explained. "Try to show that in your reports." He continued writing on the board.

"Each of you will talk for five to seven minutes. You need a bibliography of five sources."

Jared jotted down a few notes. The report was due on October 31. *Topic*, he wrote down. He drew a big question mark after that.

Mr. Wilson was droning on about topic ideas. The purple marker squeaked on the board as he wrote.

Olympics—he could do that one! He wouldn't have to do much work on that. He could talk about the U.S. National Soccer Team. Yeah, he'd have to mention Greece and that old history stuff. But he could spend most of the time talking about what he knew best—soccer.

Mr. Wilson kept printing out topics—*Socrates, Sparta, Women in Ancient Greece.*

Hmmm, Jared thought. He grinned. Women. That wouldn't be too bad. He glanced at Maribel. She was hot! But he bet Mr. Wilson didn't have a talk on hot Greek babes in mind.

Mr. Wilson finished writing. He turned to the class. "All right," he said hopefully. "Anyone want any of these? First come, first served."

Jared drew in his breath. He never raised his hand in class. He especially didn't want to be the very first hand in the air. His buddies would never let him forget it.

But he had to get that Olympics topic before anyone else did. It could save his grade. Then his parents would let him go to the San Diego tournament.

Luckily, he saw Helene and Maribel raise their hands first. From the corner of his eye, he saw the new guy José slide down in his desk.

"José?" Mr. Wilson was asking. "You can pick first, since you're new to the class." He smiled at José.

But what if José wanted his topic? Jared swallowed hard. He watched José's lips move as he read the board silently. He was sure he saw José stop reading at *Olympics.*

José took a breath. "I guess—" he began.

Jared quickly raised his hand. He couldn't believe he was doing this.

"Uh, Mr. Wilson?" he blurted out.

"Whoa!" Marcus whispered next to him, a grin on his face.

"Gotta do it," Jared said in a low voice.

"Why, Mr. Crowley, what a surprise," Mr. Wilson said. "Turning over a new leaf?"

"I'd like to do the Olympics," Jared blurted out. Did he see a look of disappointment cross José's face? Tough. *He* needed that topic.

"Fine," Mr. Wilson said, sounding pleased. "I hope you do a fine job. Your grade could use it," he added.

Don't get too excited, Jared thought. He was only going to do as much as he absolutely needed to. No sense in getting all worked up over a dumb school project. Or anything, for that matter. Life was too short. He yawned and stretched his arms out in front of him.

"Have you decided yet, José?" Mr. Wilson asked. José shook his head. "Why don't you take *Sparta?*" Mr. Wilson suggested and moved on.

After everyone got a topic, Mr. Wilson let the class begin working on their reports. Some students went to the bookshelves at the back of the room. Others thumbed through the social studies textbook.

Jared watched José turn pages in the encyclopedia. He began writing things down in his notebook. So he was a kiss-up too, Jared snorted.

Jared drew a soccer field on his paper. Then he filled it with Xs and Os. How about working up a good penalty-shot defense? Coach would like that.

19

The bell finally rang. Everyone rustled books and papers. Backpacks zipped.

"Dismissed," Mr. Wilson called out, even though half the class was already out the door.

Jared grabbed his backpack and stood up.

"Gonna go to the park and practice taking shots on goal after school?" Marcus asked.

Jared stared at Marcus. "Are you crazy?" he asked. "*Extra* practice?"

Marcus shrugged. "I just thought because Coach said—"

"Coach doesn't know what he's talking about!" Jared snapped. "I've done okay without the extra practice all season, right?" he asked. He folded his arms.

Marcus looked down at the floor. "Yeah," he replied. Then he looked back at Jared. He grinned. "Aw, who cares. You're still the top scorer in the league," he said. He bumped fists with Jared.

As Jared walked out the door, he caught a glimpse of José staring at him. Jared squared his shoulders. What was up with that guy? he wondered. José had better show him some respect, or there would be trouble.

Wednesday afternoon at practice, Jared laced up his cleats on the soccer field. Everyone was kicking balls around and getting loose.

Across the field, he saw José already stretching. He must have come early. His face was serious. José stretched his back, quads, ankles, calves, and knees, one after another. Then he stood up. He began juggling a soccer ball on his instep.

Jared snorted. Show-off. Was he trying to impress Coach? Well, it wouldn't work. Jared was going to start as center striker and be top scorer on this team. There was nothing José could do about that. The ODP *had* to be in his future.

"Come on over here," Coach announced. Jared and his teammates circled Coach.

"Let's work on shots on goal today," Coach said. "And on some defensive drills. In case we don't score as we should."

Jared hunched his shoulders. Was Coach on his case again?

"We're going to do a version of Wembley," Coach said. "Get in pairs. Two-on-two. Whichever team of two doesn't score is out. Each team that *does* score will shag balls. Then we'll repeat with all the scoring pairs on the field together until there are only two pairs left. We'll see who the top scorers are."

Jared lifted his chin. This drill was his chance to shine—and to let José know who the real shooter on this team was.

3
No Big Deal

Thud! Thud! Thud! Jared's feet pounded down the field toward the ball. He and Marcus had to score in this drill.

From the corner of his eye, he'd seen José watching him carefully as he took off. You watch! he wanted to yell at José. Watch how it's done!

"Yours!" shouted Marcus.

Across the field, Roy and Armando raced toward the ball too.

Jared closed in on the bouncing ball. He collected Coach's pass. Knocking it ahead, he twisted past Roy. The ball streaked through the grass in front of him.

"Yeah, Jared!" Marcus hollered.

Armando drove toward him, legs pumping. Jared had to pass to Marcus—fast.

"Jared!" Marcus shouted, running for the left sideline.

Jared struck a sweet volley with the outside of his right foot. It chipped high in the air, way over Armando's head. The ball spiraled toward Marcus. He chested the ball and settled it. He turned the ball wide and worked it down toward the goal.

Roy swept toward Marcus, his face grim. Marcus looked up and faked to the right.

Jared had slipped past Armando. He hustled down the sideline and broke for the 18-yard line.

THWACK! Marcus got off a crisp cross.

Yes! Jared thought. He pivoted quickly and trapped the ball with his thigh. Then he got his foot on the ball.

Suddenly, Roy was almost in his face. Now! Jared told himself. He swung his foot back and fired.

BOOM! He blasted his shot toward the far left post. He clenched his fists. Had he done it? Had he scored?

Yes! The ball thudded softly into the net, ballooning the back. Jared looked back at José on the sidelines. Take that! he wanted to shout.

"Shag balls, Jared and Marcus," Coach called. He served the next ball out.

"Nice shot," Marcus complimented as they reached the end line.

"Thanks," Jared said. He wiped his forehead with his sleeve. Now maybe Coach would get off his back about practicing shots on goal.

The drill ran on. Each nonscoring pair dropped out. The winners took their turns shagging balls.

Coach lofted the ball in the air. Standing on the end line, Jared watched José and his partner, Kevin. José's feet skimmed the grass as he ran toward the ball.

"He's fast," Marcus said, watching José.

"Yeah," Jared muttered.

Kevin bolted for the sideline. José let the ball bounce off his chest. He settled it. His opponent charged him. Coiling away from him, José neatly tapped the ball ahead.

"See me," Kevin called out.

José glanced up for an instant. His two opponents hustled toward him from the center of the field.

THWACK! José cannoned a cross to Kevin.

"Wow! Look at the foot on that guy," Marcus said.

"Yeah," Jared said. He folded his arms and watched.

Kevin dashed for the 18, dribbling the ball. José bolted away from the two defenders. He bore down on the top of the six-yard box.

"Cross!" José yelled to Kevin.

Kevin booted a floater to José. José jumped up and twisted a half-turn.

SMACK! He powered into the ball with his forehead.

Jared saw the ball arc up, heading for the goal. It swooped into the net, just under the crossbar.

"Oh, yeah," Marcus breathed. "Nice header."

"Uh-huh," Jared said through clenched teeth.

"Repeat," Coach yelled. "All five scoring pairs. Everyone on the field together. Let's see who can really score here. A little World Cup drill."

The scoring pairs clustered on the half line. Jared and Marcus stood impatiently, waiting for Coach to serve the ball.

"We have to win this," Jared muttered to Marcus.

"Yeah," Marcus agreed.

Whoosh! Coach threw in the ball. Shouts echoed across the field.

Jared set his jaw. He burst past the other pairs, racing for the ball. Keeping his body between the attackers and the ball, he trapped the ball with his shins.

Got it! he told himself. Tapping the ball, he slashed across the field. Kevin roared up, but Jared brushed by him.

"Unnnnh!" Jared grunted. Somebody charged into him from the side. He felt his feet go out from under him. Thud! He landed on his backside on the grass.

He looked up to see José scrambling to his feet. Then José flew past him, chasing the ball. It was José who had tackled him! Where had he come from?

Fuming, Jared ran toward the 18. He had to steal the ball back and score. He dodged and faked his way downfield.

BOOM!

What was that? Jared glanced back toward José. José had just sent a blistering shot right into the goal from the 18.

"Okay," Coach said. "Good work, Kevin and José. Shag balls. Everyone else keep going."

The rest of the pairs jogged back to the half line. Coach served another ball onto the field.

Time after time, Jared snagged the ball. But three of his shots went wide. Two other shots arced over the crossbar. What was wrong? he scolded himself. Maybe he needed to take more time making his shots. Maybe he was hurrying too much.

Then two other pairs scored quickly. He and Marcus were still on the field with the last pair, Jon and Kenneth.

"We can't be the big losers," Jared grumbled.

"We'll do it," Marcus said. "Don't worry about it."

Jared caught a glimpse of José's face. He was standing next to Kevin talking. The jerk was smiling. Think this is funny, huh? Jared snapped silently.

Jared made a few runs toward the goal with the ball. One shot bounced off the far post. The other sailed over the crossbar. Marcus took a shot, but it cut wide.

Kenneth snatched the next ball. He banked left, tapping the ball ahead of him.

Jared sliced toward the goal, trying to cut off the angle. Kenneth squeezed a pass to the front of the goal, right ahead of Jared to Jon.

Jared put on a burst of speed. Did he have time to push Jon off the ball?

Turning quickly, Jon sent a hard shot into the corner of the net.

Jared blinked. That was it. He and Marcus had lost. Head down, he jogged off the field.

"Okay, all the winners again," Coach said.

Jared dropped down at the edge of the field. Marcus plopped next to him.

"Not too good, huh?" Marcus mumbled.

Jared frowned. He folded his arms on his knees.

"I thought you almost had it a couple of times," Marcus said.

"Yeah?" Jared snapped. "Well, I guess not."

"Back off, okay?" Marcus warned. "It's not *me* who's the top scorer in the league."

Jared sighed and shut his eyes.

"Look at that José guy," Marcus said.

Against his will, Jared opened his eyes in time to see José run onto the bouncing ball. He ripped a right-footed volley into the net.

"Not bad," Marcus said.

Jared just sighed. Coach was going to be all over him again.

After half an hour of defensive drills, the rest of practice passed quickly.

"We're done for today, Thunder," called Coach Mulvey. "Keep up that shots-on-goal practice on our off days. And remember ball work. You have to be hungry."

Sitting on the grass, Jared unlaced his cleats. Unzipping his soccer bag, he tossed the cleats inside. Savagely, he zipped up the bag again. Next to him, Marcus stood up, brushing grass clippings off his shorts.

"Jared," Coach's voice boomed.

Jared looked up to see Coach Mulvey standing in front of him, hands on his hips.

"Uh-huh?" Jared asked. His heart sank. Coach had that "let's talk" look on his face.

"Later, bro," Marcus said quickly. He grabbed his soccer bag and walked away.

"You started off practice well today," Coach said to Jared. He paused.

"Thanks," Jared said.

"But you really lost it at the end of the World Cup drill." Coach frowned. "What's up with you lately?" he asked. "You've lost your edge in scoring. Haven't you been practicing?"

"Yeah, I have," Jared lied. No way was he going to admit he hadn't been. "I guess I just have to do more," he fibbed.

"Remember, Olympic Development Program scouts will be at the play-off game. I know how much that means to you. But if you're not scoring, I won't be playing you."

Coach glanced across the field. Jared followed his eyes. José was walking toward the parking lot with Kevin and Armando.

"There are other players who can score," Coach went on. "I never thought I'd be saying this to you, Jared. You have so much talent. I hate to see it wasted."

"Okay, Coach," Jared answered. "Don't worry. I'll do it."

"I'll start you at center striker in tomorrow's game," Coach said. "But if you don't score, I'll have no choice but to take you out," he warned.

"Yeah, I understand," Jared said. He stood up, ready to go.

"See you tomorrow," Coach finished.

Jared hurried to catch up with Marcus.

29

"What did Coach want?" Marcus asked.

"The same old stuff," Jared complained.

"Practice?" Marcus asked.

"Of course," Jared snorted. Together, they walked to the parking lot. Jared craned his neck, looking for Dad's car. "But I'm not going to spend all my free time doing soccer drills," Jared said. He shrugged. "I didn't practice a lot before. So why do I need to do it now? It's no big deal."

"Yeah," Marcus agreed. "You're right. *I*, on the other hand, *have* to practice. But then . . ." Marcus grinned. "I'm not the major talent you are!" he joked, punching Jared lightly on the shoulder.

Jared laughed, punching him back. Then his face grew serious. Major talent, he repeated silently. That major talent had better be on for tomorrow's game, he told himself.

4

The Battle Begins

"How was practice?" Dad asked when Jared opened the rear car door.

"Yeah, Jared. How many goals did you score?" taunted JoDee. She turned to face him from the front seat. "Oh, I forgot. You don't need to practice. Just us humans have to do that," she added with an evil snicker.

"Ha, ha," Jared sneered. "Of course, *you* always practice, Miss Perfect. But that's because if you don't, you'd forget how to kick the ball." Jared dropped down on the seat and leaned his head back.

"Enough," Dad growled from the driver's seat. "You two are going to drive me crazy with this bickering. If I'd known this, your mom and I wouldn't have ordered twins."

"Very funny, Dad," JoDee said. She glared at Jared. Turning around, she tossed her ponytail back.

"Practice go all right?" Dad repeated. He raised his eyebrows at Jared in the rearview mirror.

"Yeah," Jared mumbled. Sure, it had gone all right. If he didn't count Coach's little talk. Or how he'd missed those shots.

Jared shook his head to clear it. He'd show Coach and everyone in the game against the Invaders tomorrow. He *had* to—if he wanted to play center striker in the play-offs when the ODP scout was watching.

Jared settled into his social studies seat Thursday afternoon just as the bell rang.

"Ahem! Class! Class has begun," Mr. Wilson said in a high-pitched voice. "Settle down now."

Little by little, the students stopped chattering. The room grew quiet. Jared looked over at Maribel. She was even better-looking today than she had been yesterday. Maybe she'd come to the game after school if he asked her.

Then he glanced back at José. José was sitting up straight in his chair, looking at Mr. Wilson. His book and notebook were already open on the desk.

Jared snorted. What a goody-goody the guy was!

"Today we'll continue working on your oral reports," Mr. Wilson said. "I'll be around to check on your progress." He cleared his throat. "Use your time wisely," he added. "Remember the requirements."

Was Mr. Wilson warning him personally? Jared wondered. He made a face. Why was everyone on his case?

Students began working. A few whispers and giggles broke the silence.

Jared sighed. He opened his social studies book. Turning to the index at the back, he looked for "Olympics." There it was! He flipped to page 236.

Beginning as a competition between . . . Jared read silently. Boring. A real snoozer. He looked around the room. Maribel was scribbling in her notebook. A stack of books sat on her desk. Why did she work so hard? She was smart enough. She didn't have to beat it to death, Jared thought.

He leaned back in his desk. Shifting his head from side to side, he cracked his neck like he'd seen the major league soccer players do on TV. Maybe that would help him shoot better again. He sat up quickly. The game. He had to ask Maribel to come to the game.

"How is your research coming, Mr. Crowley?" Mr. Wilson's voice grated right in his ear.

Jared jerked in surprise. Research? he wanted to ask. What research?

"Mr. Crowley?" Mr. Wilson stood right next to Jared's desk. He leaned closer.

"Uh, research?" Jared blurted out.

"For your report. Bibliography? Remember? Five outside sources," Mr. Wilson said. "You need to bring up your grade. Requirements, Crowley, requirements."

"Yes, Mr. Wilson," Jared sighed. "I get it."

"See that you get it done," Mr. Wilson urged him. Then he moved on to the next student.

Five sources. Great. That was why Maribel had those books on her desk. He looked around the room. Other kids had only one book on their desk like he did.

He shrugged his shoulders. He could do some research later. Maybe he'd go to the school library. A thought popped into his mind, and he grinned. He could ask Maribel to help him.

Jared doodled some soccer plays on his paper for a while. Then he sighed. He forced himself to read about the Olympics. This would be such an easy topic, he told himself. He was so smart to have picked it. He couldn't wait to tell the class about the U.S. National Soccer Team at the Olympics. He'd even bring in pictures and junk. It would bring up his grade big-time.

"Class dismissed," Mr. Wilson announced as the bell finally rang. "Do your homework."

Jared shoved his book into his backpack. He got up quickly from his desk. Threading his way down the aisle, he worked his way toward Maribel.

But she was already talking to José. *Talking to José?* Jared steeled himself. Was this guy moving in on him everywhere?

"See you," Maribel was saying. José smiled and his face turned a deep red. Glancing at Jared, he turned and walked out the door.

"Hey," Jared said to Maribel. He watched José's back disappear through the doorway. "What's up with the new guy?" he asked, trying to sound casual.

"He just wanted some help with his report," Maribel explained. "He's not sure how to do the bibliography. He's really nice, you know. Kinda shy."

"Sure," Jared grunted. Shy? Yeah, right. The guy was moving in on his girl. Girls always went for that "shy" stuff.

Jared cleared his throat. "So, I was thinking. Were you and Helene gonna come watch the Thunder game after school?"

Maribel's smile lit up her face. "Yeah, we planned on it." She smiled up at him. "Are you gonna score your usual goals?" she asked.

Jared felt his face get warm above his collar. "You never know," he said with fake modesty. "Oh, yeah. I could use some help on my report too. With the research, you know? At the school library, maybe?" he added hopefully.

It was Maribel's turn to blush. "Of course," she said. "Maybe we can get a pass from study hall."

"Okay," Jared said. He grinned. "Thanks. See you later."

"What was all that about?" Marcus quizzed him as they walked outside. "Getting some private tutoring?" he teased.

"Nah," Jared protested. He scuffed his shoes as they walked. "I have to get a good grade on that oral report," he explained. "Or else no San Diego tournament."

"Why don't you ask *me*?" Marcus teased. "Seeing as how I'm a B student and all." He punched Jared lightly on the arm. "Why not tap *my* awesome brain?"

"Get out," Jared joked, grinning. "Maribel and Helene are coming to the game after school," he added.

"You'd better look good then, my man," Marcus said.

Later on the soccer field, Marcus jogged to his position. He took a deep breath. The field was lined with people sitting on the grass or in lawn chairs.

He could see Maribel and Helene whispering and giggling. Dad stood on the sideline at the half, his hands in his pockets. He was working the night shift this week. His mom wasn't there. She was at work.

Jared glanced back at the cluster of subs. José squatted next to Coach, staring intently at the field.

At his center striker position, Jared crouched lightly on the balls of his feet.

TWEEEET! The ref's whistle blew. Running across the midfield circle, Marcus tapped the ball back to him to start the play.

Jared collected the pass. A green-shirted Invader midfielder barreled toward him. Jared quickly sidestepped the player, cradling the ball between his feet. Then he knocked the ball wide into open space. He raced after it, dodging another Invader. Two more green shirts ran to cover him.

Jared glanced up. Were any of his teammates ready to receive a pass? Yes, Armando was open at the 18.

Jared fired a cross toward the open space. Armando neatly trapped the ball and turned it wide. He swept down the sideline toward the goal.

Now, Jared told himself. He plunged through the green-shirted defenders toward the goal's far post. At the top of the box, he turned, ready to get a cross from Armando.

A huge Invader fullback pounded up to mark him. No way, Jared told himself. He pivoted, twisting past the Invader.

BOOM! Armando's cross soared through the air. Jared focused on the spiraling ball. He jumped up and chested the ball down. Steady, he told himself. Make it work.

The Invader stopper suddenly appeared between him and the goal. Shouts floated through the air. His teammates and the crowd were yelling.

"Shot, Jared!"

"Shoot!"

SMACK! He chipped the ball up, high over the stopper's head. Please let it go in, he breathed.

The crowd groaned as the ball curled harmlessly over the crossbar. It bounced behind the goal, out-of-bounds.

At least it was a shot, Jared told himself. He quickly jogged back into position. The Invader's keeper booted the ball through the air toward the half line. Play began again.

The next 20 minutes flew by. Jared stole the ball from a midfielder and passed it to Marcus. Marcus fed it to him for another shot—and another miss.

Roy lobbed the ball forward to him. Jared slipped past a green fullback to shoot past him from close range.

BOOM! The ball smacked against the post. Another miss. Jared clenched his fists.

"Bad luck," Marcus yelled to him over his shoulder as they ran to midfield.

At least the Invaders hadn't scored either, Jared told himself. He could hardly look at the crowd though. What was Coach thinking? He groaned inwardly.

His shoulders slumped. His legs burned from his sprints toward the goal and down the field. Where was his magnet into the goal? Just a few games ago, it seemed as if he could do no wrong. Now he couldn't even net one shot.

TWEEEET! The ref's whistle blew, signaling the end of the half. Coach called them over to sit under a tree. Jared dropped to the grass with his teammates. He unscrewed the cap of his water jug. Tipping his head back, he gulped the cool water.

"We aren't scoring, Thunder," Coach said. "We need to beat this team, or we're not going to make the play-offs. We're going to make some changes." Coach looked at Jared and shook his head.

"You could use a rest, Jared," Coach commented. "Sit out for a while. José, you'll play center striker."

Marcus jabbed Jared with his elbow and raised his eyebrows.

Jared shrugged and made silent excuses. Coach would put him back in soon. José wouldn't be able to do any better.

But was he wrong. In amazement, Jared watched José work his way downfield to the goal. José got his head on a crisp pass from Armando and headed the ball into the goal.

Ten minutes later, José fired a low shot past the Invader keeper and into the net, scoring again.

A few minutes later, Marcus fell back, got his foot on the ball, and blasted a cross to José. José fired another shot just over the keeper's outstretched fingers.

The crowd roared. Jared saw his dad standing quietly, his hands still in his pockets. Maribel and Helene clapped and yelled when José scored.

Jared kept looking over at Coach. When was he going to go in again? He needed a chance to score. He'd helped make the Thunder almost undefeated, hadn't he? But Coach never looked his way.

Jared sunk his chin in his hands, glaring at the field. His teammates on the sidelines watched the game closely. They hooted and hollered each time

José scored. Jared sat in stony silence. He had to force himself to cheer after each goal.

TWEEEET! The ref's whistle was drowned in cheers. The Thunder team yelled and clapped one another on the back, bumping fists.

Fine, Jared fumed. He'd get this under control. No new guy was going to come on this team and take his position away. Not when it meant the play-offs. Not when it meant a chance of making the Olympic Development Program.

Tomorrow's practice was going to be different.

5
Hard Knocks

"Better, Crowley, better," Coach called to Jared after Friday's practice.

Jared nodded. He wiped the sweat off his forehead with his shirtsleeve. He and Marcus sat with the rest of the Thunder, stripping off their shin guards and socks. The setting sun sent long shadows across the grass.

"At least you got a few," Marcus said to him. "The old Jared could be back." He grinned. "Did you have a secret practice by yourself after the game yesterday? Trying to impress you-know-who?" he teased.

Jared felt his face turn warm. "Nah," he protested. "No extra practice. I have a life, you know." He shrugged. "My game's just been off a little lately. I'm trying to get it back. I'll do it."

"Yeah," Marcus said.

"I'm still missing some," Jared admitted. "But at least I scored today." Which was more than he'd been doing. He'd been keeping track. He'd missed three out of every four shots on goal he'd taken during practice. And José had *scored* on three out of four. Jared sighed.

"All right, Thunder," Coach Mulvey announced. "We'll see you bright and early for the game tomorrow morning. The Cyclone team is tough, but if we mark their midfielders, we should be able to contain them. As far as our scoring," Coach went on. Then he stopped and looked at José.

What? Jared wanted to blurt out.

"We're getting closer to the play-offs and our game against the Sting," Coach continued. "We need to be aggressive. I'm going to start José at center striker tomorrow. Jared, you'll play left wing."

Jared felt Marcus jab him. Jared narrowed his eyes.

"No way that's gonna last," Jared muttered. He jerked his head toward José.

Marcus raised his eyebrows. "Whoever scores, right?" he asked.

Jared felt anger throb behind his eyes. Was even Marcus turning on him?

"I can score!" Jared snapped. "I just have to feel it again." He stood up and grabbed his soccer bag. "See ya," he said.

Jared strode across the grass. Before he started up the steps, he stopped. He turned to look back at the field. José was squatting on his haunches talking to Marcus. Jared saw them bump fists and laugh. He stared unblinkingly for a second. Then he walked to the car, gripping the handles of the soccer bag tightly. He flung open the car door.

"Hi," Dad said from the front seat. Jared looked inside the car. Whew! Joad the Toad wasn't there. She must not have had practice today. At least he'd get some peace on the way home.

"Did you do better today?" Dad asked. He started up the car.

"Uh-huh," Jared muttered. He clicked the seat belt buckle hard. Better? Did *everyone* think he needed improvement?

"Coach Mulvey talked with me after the game yesterday. He wants you to practice taking shots more often," Dad said. They pulled out of the parking lot.

Jared felt his blood beginning to boil.

"Oh, yeah?" he snapped. "Let Coach take practice shots. I get plenty of practice." He turned his face toward the window.

"Coach says you've always had natural talent," Dad went on. "But the competition level is higher now. You need to get more serious." He glanced at Jared.

"I'm serious enough," Jared muttered. He wasn't going to turn into one of those weird, intense guys who only cared about soccer. Yeah, he wanted to play pro soccer, but he had enough talent to do that without beating his brains out practicing night and day.

Jared warmed up on the sidelines before the game on Saturday morning. He stretched his quads. Then he began rotating his ankles. Next to him, Marcus grunted as he stretched.

"*Hola*, Marcus," a voice said. Jared looked over. José stood in front of Marcus, cradling a soccer ball between his feet. He flicked the ball up on top of his thigh. Tap, tap, tap—he juggled the ball from his instep to his thigh.

Show-off, Jared snorted silently.

"Thanks for taking shots with me yesterday after practice," José said in a low voice.

"No problem," Marcus said. He glanced at Jared quickly. Jared turned away, pretending to stretch his back. But he listened carefully.

"I am nervous about today," José said. "I mean, about starting." He shrugged. "The team really wants to win. I'll have to work hard. *Trabajo como burro*," he joked.

"You'll score," Marcus assured him.

You'll score, Jared repeated silently. When was the last time Marcus—or anyone—had said those words to *him*? Jared grumbled to himself. Whose team was this anyway?

The game began. The Thunder came out running, making accurate passes. José scored twice in the first half. He fired a line drive at the goal, right past the keeper. For the second goal, he headed off a soft, high corner kick. He got his head on it and knocked it over the keeper's outstretched fingers.

Jared got off a few shots from left wing, but the ball zoomed over the crossbar or bounced off the posts each time. The keeper leaped and punched his last shot over the crossbar. Jared wanted to boot the ball right into the keeper's smug face.

TWEEEET! The ref's whistle blew to signal halftime. Jared jogged to the sideline and plopped on the grass. Reaching for his thermos, he twisted open the cap. He gulped water noisily. Sweat glued his shirt to his back. He pulled out his shirttail, mopping his forehead with it. His chest pounded from racing up and down the field.

Coach cleared his throat. "Good half, Thunder. Nice marking, defense," he said. "José, you're consistent in your shots on goal." Jared saw Armando and Ivan reach across to bump fists with José. A slow smile crossed José's face.

Coach was still talking. "Marcus, well-timed crosses. Chas, good work at sweeper. Nice tackles."

And where was *his* name? Jared wondered. He'd been working hard too.

"Jared, take a break. I'll play Ivan at left wing," Coach finished. "Get plenty of water."

Jared flexed his fingers. He couldn't believe this!

Play began again after the ref's whistle. The Thunder pulled the Cyclone defenders out of position. From his place on the sideline, Jared saw Ivan cross the ball to José. José sent a blistering pass into the goal. The keeper dove for it, missing it by a mile.

When was he going to get back in the game? Jared stared at Coach. But Coach's eyes were on the field. Jared's stomach tightened. This wasn't happening.

The final whistle was drowned in cheers. The game was over. The Thunder had won with a score of 4 to 1.

Jared got up slowly. He joined his teammates already celebrating in the center of the field.

"Nice game, José!" Kenneth was saying.

"Great header," Ramon called out, clapping José on the back.

Jared gritted his teeth. He went through the motions of slapping the Cyclone's hands.

"Good game, good game," he muttered. A good game, he repeated silently. They needed to play a good game—no, a *great* game—against the Sting on Thursday. They had to win to get to the play-offs. Would he even be *in* the game?

Jared sulked in the car on the way home.

"Move over!" he snapped at Joad the Toad, who was already sitting in the backseat. He shoved her soccer bag on the floor.

"What's the matter, Jared?" JoDee taunted him. "Get your feelings hurt today? You're not the scoring stud anymore?" She grinned evilly at him, crinkling up her eyes.

"Coach decide you needed a rest?" Mom asked from the front seat.

"Yeah," Jared mumbled. He stared out the window.

"Wouldn't have anything to do with your not scoring the first half, would it?" Dad asked. He looked at Jared in the rearview mirror.

"I don't know," Jared muttered. A frown creased his forehead.

"I think you *do* know," Dad said.

"Back off, will you?" Jared snapped. He clenched his fists. "Just leave me alone."

"Whoa, there, son," Dad said. "You watch your attitude. You're on a slippery slope here."

"Everyone's on my back," Jared complained.

"Just bite the bullet and practice," Dad said. "You know what Coach said."

"And that kind of attitude will keep you from going to San Diego," Mom warned. "Even if you *do* bring up your social studies grade."

"Right," JoDee crowed. She tossed her hair back and smirked.

"JoDee, you stay out of this," Mom said. "You're on thin ice yourself."

JoDee hunched her shoulders. She slid down in her seat. "Yes, Mom," she sighed. Then she shot a mean look at Jared.

At least Joad the Toad might shut up for a few seconds now, Jared consoled himself. But what about everyone else? He slumped against the back of the seat.

49

On Monday, Jared sat in social studies watching the clock. The hands crawled slowly around the dial. Everyone was working. Whispers and the sounds of pencil scratchings filled the air. He stared at the book and papers on his desk and sighed.

He looked around for Maribel. Her desk was empty. She was kneeling in front of the bookshelves at the back of the room. Open books lay on the floor in front of her.

Glancing at Mr. Wilson at the front of the room, Jared got up. He figured now was a good time to go talk to Maribel. He looked at José sitting in the back row. Would José try to move in on Maribel now?

But José's eyes were on his work. Three books sat on his desk. An open notebook and papers were scattered next to them. Jared frowned.

"Hey, what's up?" Jared asked Maribel. He squatted down next to her.

She smiled at him. "Just doing some research on my project," she replied. "I heard you won Saturday," she added.

No thanks to me, Jared thought. "Yeah," he managed to say.

"José can really score," she said.

"Uh-huh," Jared said. "Anyway, we're playing the Sting on Thursday. If we beat them, we go to the play-offs," he added.

"Maybe I'll come to the game," Maribel said. "Will you score some goals for me?" she teased, her dimples flashing.

Jared felt his face turn warm. "I don't know— maybe," he hedged.

"Mr. Crowley?" Mr. Wilson's voice called from the front of the room. "If you're not going to do your own work, don't keep others from doing theirs."

"I'd better go," Jared whispered, rolling his eyes at Mr. Wilson.

Maribel giggled. Her warm brown eyes sparkled at him.

Maybe he'd at least get the girl if he couldn't get the game, Jared tried to comfort himself. He dropped down into his seat.

But he wanted the game too—even more than the girl. He wanted to score the winning goal against the Sting. And he wanted to be the best player in the play-offs. He wanted to be the player the ODP scout would watch.

Today at practice, he would work hard. *Trabajo como burro*, as José would say. Then Coach would play him against the Sting at center striker.

Besides, José probably couldn't handle the Sting's playing style. They fought dirty. All the other teams knew that. The Sting slide-tackled their opponents from behind when the ref wasn't watching. In fact, the team had a whole bagful of illegal moves and hits. Jared and the Thunder knew what to expect. The Sting had been the only team to beat them this season.

There was no way José could be ready for that, Jared snorted to himself. Maribel had said José was "kinda shy." Well, "shy" wouldn't cut it in a game against the Sting.

But first he needed to take care of today's practice. He'd focus hard. He'd show Coach he could score. He would make a comeback.

6

No Way!

Monday's practice was almost over. His legs burning from runs at the goal, Jared dropped down on the grass. Sweat dripped off his forehead. His eyes stung. He rubbed his face with his shirtsleeve.

"Get some water," Coach directed. "Then we'll run 'the weave.'

"You know what we're up against with the Sting," Coach continued. "This drill will help. We have to use our open space creatively on the field. We can't rely on only one player to do all our scoring. Otherwise they'll just mark him and take him down when he has the ball."

No joke! Jared told himself. He glanced at José. He could already see José lying on the field moaning in pain after a Sting slide tackle. The Sting would make José pay for his shots on goal. He wouldn't even know what had hit him.

Armando and Kevin sat on either side of José. José and Kevin had just won the World Cup drill Coach ran. They won it *again*, Jared reminded himself angrily. He retied his soccer cleats, yanking the laces hard.

Coach looked at Jared. "Jared, you'll match up with José and Kevin."

He was teamed with José? Jared held back a frown. He wanted to shine on his own. Now he'd have to cooperate with the new hotshot.

Coach went on. "Armando—you, Roy, and Marcus will team up. Ivan, Kenneth, and Jon, you'll be together. Everyone else on defense—midfielders and fullbacks. Ramon, you'll be keeper. Rory will spell you off. Now use the open space. Remember, take over the space left by the player who has the ball. Let's go!"

Jared jogged to the half line. He'd take the center position, his old position. Kevin took the left wing spot. José moved into right wing. The defenders took their places.

TWEEEET! Coach blew his whistle, throwing the ball to Jared. Kevin and José sprinted for the alleys, looking for open space.

Jared knocked the ball forward. He gave a head fake to Ernesto, as if he were going to pass it right. Then he turned the ball wide and angled a pass left to Kevin, who'd found open space near the left sideline.

Quickly, Jared raced to switch places with Kevin. He pivoted around Chas and ground his way down the left sideline.

Now Kevin was dribbling down the center of the field. Challenged by KeShaun, Kevin sent a hard cross up to José. José was open near the 18 in the right alley. Then Kevin ran to switch with José, who worked the ball back to the center again.

Chest pounding, Jared found himself at the left corner of the six-yard box. No defenders challenged him. Robert was pulled way out of position at full. Jared could score if José passed to him.

José glanced over at Jared as he ran. José was closing in on the goal, the ball flashing black and white between his feet. Would José pass to him? Or would he try to shoot himself? Jared almost held his breath.

FLICK! José curled a soft floater in Jared's direction. Yes! Jared thought. He settled the ball with his thigh. He heard Chas closing in behind him, breath ragged.

BOOM! Jared booted the ball toward the far post.

SMACK! The ball cannoned off the post, bouncing clear over the sideline. Ramon jogged to retrieve it.

Jared wanted to punch his fist right through the net.

Kevin, José, and Jared turned and jogged back to the half line. José ran next to Jared.

"How about trying a header?" José asked. "A header would have worked, *no?*"

"Yeah," Jared muttered through clenched teeth. He stared straight ahead as he ran.

"I'll practice headers with you sometime," José offered. They reached the half line.

"I'm too busy," Jared retorted. He forced himself to keep his voice level. From the corner of his eye, he saw José shrug. Jared turned to watch the action begin again with the next three players.

Jared's hands shook with anger. What a jerk! José acted as if he were Pele or Maradona or Zidane or somebody. What was he thinking? Did he think he was going to show Jared how to score? Jared wanted to punch his smug face. He stared intently at the next players running the drill.

Blood was still pounding in his forehead when it was his turn again. Coach served the ball to him at the half.

Jared streaked past KeShaun, who was covering him. He looked ahead. José was in the clear in the right alley. All right, he snapped silently, let's see you work *this* ball.

"José!" Jared yelled.

Jared sent a solid pass toward José. How's that for a floater? he wanted to shout.

José trapped it neatly with his chest. He chipped the ball ahead into midfield.

Jared hustled to take José's place on the right. Jared faked his way past a fullback, twisting to leave him in the dust. He put on a burst of speed, closing in on the right side of the penalty area.

Legs pumping, Kevin kept working his way down the left sideline.

José gained yardage down the center of the field. He dodged one defender, then another. He lofted the ball in an accurate cross to Kevin. Then he took Kevin's place on the left, slipping past a fullback.

Kevin quickly drove the ball toward the center. He raced toward the six-yard box. He looked up to see Jared open at the top of the box.

Jared glanced across the field. José was in perfect position at the far post. Which one would Kevin choose?

He got his answer as Kevin lobbed a high volley toward José. José leaped up. His forehead met the ball.

SMACK! Jose headed the ball into the goal in a perfect arc. Ramon jumped up to bat the ball away. But he was a second too late. The back of the net ballooned with the shot.

Kevin and José yelled. They bumped fists. Jared stalked over to join them.

He bumped fists with José and Kevin. "Nice pass," he said to Kevin. He just stared at José.

Then he turned to jog back to the half line, his face burning in humiliation. Now his own teammates didn't even trust him. Kevin had passed off to José. That would never have happened before José joined the team.

Jared was still fuming when Coach called an end to practice. The team bunched together on the grass, drinking from water jugs and mopping their foreheads. Jared found a place next to Marcus. Marcus nodded at him.

"Well, Thunder, you should be ready for the Sting on Thursday," Coach said. "You made good use of your open space in the drill. Nice shooting, José. Good crosses, Kevin."

Coach's glance flickered on Jared for an instant. And? Jared wanted to shout. What about him?

"We'll see you at practice Wednesday," Coach continued. "It'll be a short one. I don't want you to be exhausted for the game the next day.

"Do your ball work," Coach added. "And take shots on goal. Now get on home." He looked at Jared. "Hold on there a minute, Crowley. I want to talk with you."

Jared's heart hammered. What did Coach want now? Marcus got up quickly and walked over to Armando. They began talking about the upcoming game.

"Listen," Coach said in a low voice, "I'm not going to play you at center striker against the Sting."

Jared felt as if he were listening to Coach underwater. The words pushed themselves into his brain and echoed back and forth. He swallowed hard.

"You just aren't scoring like you used to," Coach said. He shook his head. "What happened to all that talent?" he asked. "You'll be a midfielder on Thursday. Just feed the ball to the strikers. Use your foot for those crosses. Take any opportunities you can get to shoot. But be unselfish."

Coach sighed. "The only other thing I can do is bench you completely. But that wouldn't help the team." He began to walk away but then turned to face Jared again. "I hope you get it together, Jared," he finished.

Stunned, Jared sat in silence for a second. Marcus walked over.

"Ready?" Marcus asked. His eyes searched Jared's face.

Jared grunted, keeping his eyes on the ground.

Marcus pulled Jared to his feet. Together, they walked across the field. Jared's head felt stuffed with cotton. Coach's words still rang in his head.

"We'll beat the Sting," Marcus said. "With José scoring so many goals, we should kill them."

Jared couldn't believe his ears. He scuffed his soccer slip-ons in the grass as they walked. His mouth tightened.

"So," Marcus said, "why don't you take some extra practice with me and José tomorrow after school?"

Jared gritted his teeth in anger. "I'm busy," he choked out. "And I'm just in a little slump," he added. "I'll get it back. It's no big deal."

Marcus just looked at him, his eyebrows raised. Then he shrugged. "Whatever," he said.

No way was he going to practice with José, Jared told himself. Then he sighed. He had to face it. Maybe he did have to practice after all. But he didn't have to do it with José!

He'd practice a little tomorrow after school. Not much—just a little. All he had to do was get his edge back. He had to find that "net magnet" he used to have.

No way was José going to be the top scorer of the Thunder. No way was Jose going to be the star of the play-off game. No way was José going to be scouted for the ODP instead of him.

New Hope

The bell rang, ending social studies class the next afternoon. Jared zipped up his backpack. Another hour wasted. He made a face. This Olympics topic wasn't as easy as he'd thought it was going to be. Too much stuff had happened in the Greek Olympics.

Jared sighed. Maybe he could give a quick summary of the old Greek junk from the textbook. Then he'd fill up the rest of the five minutes with all the stuff about the U.S. Olympic Soccer Team. Would that work? Would that get him the grade he needed?

The report was due next Monday. This was already Tuesday. Jared frowned. There was too much going on in his life right now—soccer problems, his parents hassling him, Joad the Toad bugging him. And he had less than a week to get a good grade on his report—or no San Diego trip.

Jared got up from his desk. He'd talk to Maribel on the way out the door. Maybe she could go to the library with him tomorrow during study hall. She hadn't been able to go last time.

"Hey, Maribel," he said, walking fast to catch up with her. He glanced over his shoulder at José. José was talking to Mr. Wilson. Figures, Jared snorted.

"Hi," Maribel said, smiling. Together, they walked out the door.

"Do you think you can go with me to the library tomorrow?" Jared asked. "During study hall? To help me with my report?"

A worried crease appeared on Maribel's forehead. "Um, sure. I'd like to. But just for a short time, okay?" she asked. "I still have so much to do on my own report. My parents are on me to keep up my grades." She smiled apologetically. "You know how it is," she added.

"Yeah, I do," Jared said. Except his parents weren't on him to keep straight As. They got really excited when he brought home anything above a C.

"Thanks," Jared said. "See you tomorrow."

He nodded quickly to Marcus across the room. Then Jared hurried out of the classroom. He walked quickly down the hall and out of the main school doors before Marcus could catch up with him. He didn't want Marcus to ask him to practice with him and José again.

He was going to keep his promise to himself. Today he would take a couple of soccer balls to the park. He'd take a million shots on goal. *Trabajo como burro.* Then they'd see who would be the center striker on the Thunder again.

He hopped off the bus in front of the apartment. Would there be any kids kicking balls around at the park? he wondered. Would they shag balls for him? He couldn't count on that.

He didn't want anyone on the Thunder to know he was worried enough to practice. So asking one of his teammates for help was out.

He rolled his eyes. He'd have to ask Joad the Toad to shag for him. Jared held back a groan. Was it worth it?

He let himself in with his key. Mom would be at work. Dad had a day shift today. So it would be just him and JoDee. He grimaced. Could he beg his sister for help?

Then a picture flashed across his brain. It was José kicking the winning goal in the play-off game. Everyone cheered. The ODP scout rushed over to sign José up.

No, Jared commanded himself. That wouldn't happen. He'd have to ask JoDee to shag. Ugh!

JoDee was on the phone. "Are you kidding me?" she was squealing. "He didn't say that!" She giggled hysterically.

Jared shook his head. It was hard to believe that JoDee was one of the toughest soccer players on her girls' team. She was an all-star keeper. But no one could tell that from listening to her talk to her friends.

JoDee looked up at him. "Guess who's home?" she said into the phone. "The soccer stud!" She screeched with laughter.

Jared flung his backpack on the couch. "Ha, ha," he sneered. "Get off the phone. I have a question for you."

"I'm not getting off the phone for you," JoDee hissed, covering the mouthpiece. She listened for a second. "Oh, okay, Maria. Good luck. Call me later." She hung up the phone and turned to Jared. "Lucky for you, Maria had to baby-sit her brothers."

She should come over here and baby-sit *you*, Jared wanted to blurt out. Any other time, he would have said it. But he had to stay on JoDee's good side today—if she had one.

"Do you have a few minutes?" Jared asked. He flinched. He couldn't believe he was asking Joad the Toad for anything.

JoDee put her hands on her hips. "What is it? Need help with your report for Wilson's class?" She smirked. "Mine's almost finished. Maribel and I have been working on ours together." Her eyes gleamed wickedly. "I sure wish we were in the same social studies class. I'd love to watch you make a fool of yourself in front of everyone."

"Gee, thanks," Jared said sarcastically. "Nah," he went on quickly, "it's not about social studies." He took a deep breath. "How would you like to work on your goal keeping at the park?"

"What?" JoDee scoffed. She began to hoot with laughter. "How dumb do you think I am? Are you gonna take shot practice? *You*? The great soccer stud? The 'I'm so good I don't need to practice' starting center striker?" She giggled hysterically. "Oh, that's right, you aren't the starting center anymore, are you?

"Fine," Jared snapped. "I don't have time for this." He began to turn away. But he knew JoDee wouldn't pass up a chance to hassle him when he missed shots.

JoDee got up, still grinning. "Okay. Okay. I'll do it. But only because I really *do* need to practice my punches." She flipped her hair over her shoulder. "*If* you get anywhere near the goal, that is," she taunted.

After an hour of practice, Jared and JoDee collected the soccer balls. They shoved them into their bag. Jared wiped the sweat from his forehead. JoDee stripped off her keeper gloves. She stuffed them next to the soccer balls.

Jared began walking across the sidewalk. JoDee followed.

"It's just focus," she said, mopping her face with a sleeve. "Sometimes you just rush right into the shot. But when you took that extra second, you scored— sometimes anyway!" She grinned. "Too bad I'm such a great keeper," she added.

"Yeah, right," Jared said. But she was right about his scoring. He'd been keeping track. He'd made almost two out of every three shots. Joad the Toad had punched some of them away, but at least his shots had been in the goal.

Jared walked across the street toward their block. Now he was ready for the game Thursday. And at tomorrow's practice, he'd do better. Maybe Coach would change his mind about the Sting game on Thursday. Maybe he'd end up playing center striker after all.

Back home, he grabbed a snack and plopped on the sofa. He flipped on the TV with the remote.

"I see Mr. Responsibility is going to work on his great report now," Joad the Toad teased. "See you later," she added. She slammed the door of her room.

Jared picked up an old video of World Cup soccer matches. He slid it in the VCR. Maybe he could get some ideas for the report, he told himself.

He watched the final 1998 match between Brazil and France. Hunched on the sofa, he watched Zinedine Zidane score twice in normal time in a final. It had been the first time in 40 years, since Pele had first set the record.

Jared had seen the video a hundred times. But he still watched in excitement when Petit curled a kick to the far post and Zidane headed it home.

Later, Jared sat at the kitchen counter where Mom had set dinner down. JoDee sat next to him.

"How was school today?" Mom asked. She served herself some casserole.

"Great," JoDee bubbled. "I got an A on my English paper!" She turned and made a face at Jared.

"That's wonderful, dear," Mom said. She looked at Jared. "How about you?"

Jared stared at his plate. "It was okay as usual." Maybe he could get out of having to say anything more.

"How is your social studies report coming?" Mom asked.

Jared swallowed hard. "Uh, okay," he fibbed.

"Yeah, for all the time you're spending on it," Joad the Toad jeered.

"Put a sock in it, will you?" Jared barked out. His face turned red. "Mind your own business!"

JoDee tightened her mouth and glanced at Mom.

"Listen, Jared," Mom said. Her eyebrows knit into a frown. "Leave your sister alone. If you put the same energy into your soccer and schoolwork as you do yelling at your sister, you'd do better." She put her fork down on her plate. "And remember that San Diego is out of the picture unless your social studies grade comes up."

"Yes, Mom," Jared mumbled. "I know." He shoved a forkful of casserole into his mouth. He'd love to dump his whole plate on Joad the Toad's head. But that wouldn't get him where he wanted to go, especially to San Diego.

Besides, after his practice session today, he was sure all his problems were solved. He couldn't wait for practice tomorrow.

8
The Answer?

After Wednesday's practice, Jared sat on the edge of the field. Yanking off his shin guards, he threw them at his soccer bag.

If only he could forget what had just happened in practice. During the half-field scrimmage, hardly anyone had passed to him. And his shots . . . Jared winced. His shots on goal had been lousy.

He looked around. The rest of his teammates were laughing and talking together. They unlaced cleats and stripped off shin guards.

"We'll kill the Sting tomorrow," Marcus said. "We'll be in the play-offs for sure."

"No kidding," Armando joked. He clapped José on the back. "We have a scoring machine now."

Jared's mouth tightened.

"All right, Thunder," Coach Mulvey said. "Listen up."

The group fell silent.

"You all know how aggressively the Sting plays. Tomorrow they'll go after our top scorers," Coach warned.

Top scorers, Jared grumbled to himself. That sure wouldn't be him. Coach's words faded into the background. Jared sat lost in thought.

He'd blasted shot after shot during drills. But too many had curled over the crossbar. Or they'd gone wide. Or they'd been stopped by Ramon and Rory.

Then during the scrimmage, no one had passed to him. They'd all passed to José and Marcus. Why hadn't his teammates passed off to him?

Coach was finishing his talk. "So don't be intimidated by the Sting. You can play tough. Charge them. Be aggressive. They'll back off. We need to win this. We need to get to the play-offs. Don't let the Sting spoil that for us."

Jared sneaked a look at José. José's face wore a frown. Was he worried about playing the Sting?

Jared wondered if José had ever played against a team as rough as the Sting. Maybe he'd never been targeted with a lot of slide tackles.

Jared almost crossed his fingers for luck. Who knew what might happen in the game tomorrow? If José couldn't handle the pressure, Coach would take him out. Then Coach would put Jared in at center striker.

Even in his scoring slump, he was still the best striker on the Thunder, Jared told himself. Marcus, Kevin, Jon, Kenneth, and Ivan were good. But they still never took as many shots on goal as he did.

It would be his chance to shine. He'd be back in the game. His team would be behind him. They'd have to be. Jared doubled up his fists. He couldn't wait to see what would happen with the Sting.

"Get plenty of rest," Coach finished. "Now get out of here," he said with a grin.

Jared got up and grabbed his soccer bag. Kevin and José walked across the field. Marcus and Roy waited for Jared.

But Jared motioned for them to go on. He didn't feel like talking to anyone. He needed to get his head back into scoring. That was what he needed. Practice hadn't ever helped him before. It was all in his head. It had to be.

"Jared?" Coach's voice called.

Jared looked up. He held back a sigh. Here it came—another lecture.

He walked over to Coach. Coach slapped his clipboard against his thigh.

"What's going on, Jared?" Coach asked.

"Aw, nothing," Jared mumbled. "I just have to get my head back into scoring, that's all."

"Have you been practicing?" Coach asked.

"Yeah. Yeah, I have," Jared said uneasily. Coach didn't have to know it was only yesterday.

"Your sense of touch and your timing are off," Coach said. "I watched you during the drills today." He frowned. "Your balance is fine, but your concentration seems to slip. More practice will cure touch and timing. And," he sighed, "focusing will help your concentration. That comes from practice too."

"Uh-huh," Jared said quickly. "I know. I just have to get my head straight. It used to be okay." He shrugged. "I just don't know what's happened."

"Remember, this league is a more intense level of competition. It changes the way the game is played," Coach said. "We've talked about this before. The pace of play is faster. We don't have time to think and plan ahead during the game as much. That's why shot practice outside is so important." Jared flinched. "It will help you react quickly to a new game situation."

"Yeah, Coach," Jared said. "I know."

"I hope you keep up the outside practice," Coach said. "I hate to see all that talent wasted." He sighed. "With both you and José as strikers, the Thunder could be deadly. I'd like to start you at center, but I'm sure you understand why I can't. I have to think of the team. Because of that, I'm going to bench you for the Sting game on Saturday."

Jared felt fury bubble up. That was unfair! He clenched his fists.

"I can't think of any other way to make my point. Your teammates have lost confidence in you. They're not passing to you. So keep practicing. Get your head back in the game. If you get your scoring back, we'll need you in San Diego." Coach clapped him on the back. "See you tomorrow."

"Sure, Coach," Jared managed to blurt out. "See ya." He walked across the field.

See you at the game—but not on the field, he wanted to spit out. Unless José got mashed by the Sting.

The next afternoon, Dad drove Jared to the field for warm-ups before the game.

"I'll bet you're looking forward to the game," Dad said. He grinned. "I know how you like to rough up the Sting if you can."

"Uh, yeah," Jared mumbled. He didn't have the guts to tell Dad he wouldn't be starting—or even playing.

"So how's the new kid doing? The striker—what's his name?" Dad asked.

"José," Jared said. He tried to keep his voice level.

"So where does Coach Mulvey have him playing?" Dad asked.

Jared slid down in his seat. "Ah, he'll be starting at center striker," he choked out.

"What?" Dad exclaimed. "What about you?"

"Coach will put me in later," Jared fibbed.

Dad frowned. "I have the feeling this has to do with your lack of practice," he said. He glanced over at Jared. "Is that right?"

Jared's forehead throbbed. "No, Dad," he spluttered. "I just can't score like I used to. I have to get my head back into it, that's all."

"We'll see," Dad said. He sighed. "I thought soccer was more important to you than that. Not everything in life comes easy. Not even scoring like you used to."

Jared felt his muscles tense. No one understood. No one. Besides, the Sting would run all over José. Then he'd show all of them.

TWEEEET! The ref's whistle started the game. Sitting on the sideline, Jared watched José. His feet skimmed the grass, leaving the Sting defenders a step behind. Jared could see their stunned faces.

José zigged and zagged toward the far post. Roy and Marcus got off a couple of crisp passes, moving the ball down the field. Jared could see Sting players shoving and charging into his teammates. The ref always seemed to have his back turned. One of the Sting fullbacks earned a yellow card. But that was all. No one got a red card.

The first 15 minutes passed quickly. The ball was down in the Sting's end of the field most of the time. The Sting made a few runs at the Thunder goal, but KeShaun and Ernesto headed them off.

THWACK! Marcus sent a cross spiraling toward the far post.

BOOM! José leaped up and headed Marcus's cross into the goal.

The crowd cheered. The Thunder yelled and ran to high-five José.

He'd already scored! Jared exclaimed to himself. But it wouldn't be long before the Sting would take care of José. Then he'd be dust.

The Sting keeper hurled the ball onto the field to begin play again. Jared narrowed his eyes. The Thunder burst from their positions. Snagging the ball, Ivan and Roy made some runs, but the Sting defense was too solid for them. The Sting fullbacks marked the other strikers. Roy and Ivan had midfielders dogging their every move.

Finally, Ivan knocked the ball forward. Then he ran it down. He booted it hard to José at the 18. No one was marking José.

Jared sank his chin in his hands. José seemed to be able to twist and dodge away from every Sting defender. When were they going to attack him?

THUD! There! The Sting sweeper slide-tackled José, one leg outstretched. The sweeper tumbled down on to the field. José smacked down next to him. The loose ball spun away. For a second, no one challenged the ball. It seemed as if no one could believe what had happened.

Hah! Jared told himself. Now watch. José would be afraid. Jared almost smirked to himself.

"*Arriba!*" José shouted. He scrambled to his feet. Legs churning, José powered past a Sting fullback. He raced to the ball. Getting it under control, he forced his way toward the goal line. He turned and pivoted through the Sting defense as if they were invisible.

In disbelief, Jared watched José send a scorching shot right into the back of the net. The Sting keeper made a dive for the ball, but he missed it by a mile.

The crowd erupted in cheers.

"Way to score, *amigo*!" Armando yelled.

"Don't let them get to you," Kevin encouraged.

Gloom settled over Jared. It looked as if even the Sting couldn't throw José off his game.

The game sped by, and Jared could only watch from the sidelines. Subs came and went, since the Sting kept taking down his teammates. All the other subs got in, but not Jared.

José carried the game forward. The Sting made a wall to defend against a penalty shot from José. But José back-heeled the ball sideways to Marcus. Marcus struck his shot to the left of the wall to score.

More Sting players slide-tackled José. Three times, he fell to the ground. But each time, he jerked himself to his feet. The Sting defenders were no match for him. He ghosted through the fullbacks, ready to receive crosses from the other strikers.

Jared shook his head. The Sting scored on a cross after a long throw-in. Their center striker booted in another goal at the end of the first half. But at the end of the game, the score was Sting–2, Thunder–4. And José had scored three of the Thunder's goals. For every shot he'd made, he'd taken many more. The Sting's rough play hadn't even bothered him.

Jared dragged himself up off the grass to join his teammates in the line of high fives after the game. The Thunder players were grinning and hooting, clapping one another on the back.

Jared looked at his friends. Their uniforms were grass-stained and muddy. Sweat dripped down their faces. Jared was still in a crisp, clean uniform. He glanced around. How many people had noticed he hadn't even gotten in the game?

"Great game, José," Roy called out.

"Way to shoot," Kevin said. He bumped fists with José.

"Well done, José, well done." Coach Mulvey's voice carried from the end of the line. "Looks like we have a good chance to make the play-offs."

Jared narrowed his eyes. That was it. If all anyone cared about was scoring, then that's what he'd do. He'd become a scoring machine.

They were playing the Lasers on Saturday. The Lasers were last in the league. Jared snorted. Coach would probably play him against the Lasers. Coach would figure the Thunder could still beat them, even with Jared at center striker. Jared shook his head in disgust.

So on Saturday, he'd take the ball down the field all by himself. No one would pass to him anyway. No one had any confidence in him. Well, he'd score and show them all. Ball hog, here we come, he told himself.

That would be the answer.

9
Out of Line

"Too bad, son," Dad said, when Jared yanked open the car door.

Jared just grunted. He flung his soccer bag over the backseat.

"We have just enough time to catch the last half of JoDee's game," Dad said. He steered the car out of the parking space.

Great, Jared complained silently. He'd get to watch Joad the Toad's team win another one. And she'd brag all the way home about her saves in the goal.

Jared slumped down in his seat. The parking lot was filled with players and families getting into their cars. He watched his teammates laugh and call out to one another. Guys kept bumping fists with José and clapping him on the back. They used to do that to *him*, he grumbled.

"What's your plan to get back in the game?" Dad asked. He turned the car onto the main street.

"Just play my game," Jared muttered.

"Don't you think you'd better figure out what that is?" Dad said. He glanced at Jared.

"Leave me alone," Jared snapped. "If everybody wants a scoring machine, then that's what I'll be," he finished.

Saturday morning was cold and sunny. The team stretched and warmed up.

"Thunder?" Coach called out from behind the sideline. He motioned them over. "Let's get ready."

Jared almost held his breath. Would Coach put him in? He joined his teammates.

"The Lasers aren't much of a threat," Coach said. "They've lost most of their games. But we still have to beat them. Next Thursday, we play the Hurricane.

That's the last team we have to beat to make the play-offs against the Sting."

He looked around at the team's faces. "Let's work on our strategy. Especially our defense for corner kicks and penalty shots." Coach paused. "We have our scoring down pretty well."

Jared's heart sank. Maybe Coach wouldn't put him in. Maybe he wouldn't have a chance to prove he could be a scoring machine again. He forced himself not to look at José. The jerk was probably smiling. Nah, even José wouldn't do that.

"So let's play hard." Coach stared right at Jared. "Crowley?" he asked. "Why don't you start at center striker today?"

Jared nodded. He tried to hold back a grin. Now was his chance! If no one was going to pass to him, he'd just take the ball himself. He'd score without any help.

"Take shots," Marcus encouraged him as they jogged to their positions. Jared clenched his fists. Since when was Marcus giving *him* advice?

TWEEEET! The ref's whistle blew.

Roy tapped the ball back to Marcus. Marcus plunged across the half line, dribbling the ball. Jared raced down the field. He kept glancing over his shoulder. Was Marcus watching him? Was Marcus going to pass to him?

Marcus dodged a Laser midfielder. He lofted a pass to Ivan. Ivan tried to settle it with his thigh. Instead, the ball bounced off his thigh and spun through the air. Ivan darted toward it. He got a foot on it and knocked it off a Laser. The ball shot out-of-bounds.

TWEEEET! The ref called for a Thunder throw-in. The Thunder offense jockeyed for position.

See me! Jared wanted to call out to Ivan. He wanted the throw-in. Then he would take the ball down and score.

Ivan grabbed the ball. He stood still for a second and glanced around at the players.

Jared shoved against a Laser. No one was going to keep him from getting this ball.

Kenneth crouched in the next clear space. No way, Jared told himself. Kenneth was *not* going to get this throw-in.

Holding the ball high behind his head, Ivan took two quick steps toward the sideline. He grunted and threw the ball in. It veered toward Kenneth.

Jared leaped up and chested the ball down. Getting control, he began twisting his way around the surprised Lasers.

The far post! The far post! Jared commanded himself. He shifted to the left around a Laser fullback. The ball spun in front of him. He pounded down the field toward the goal. Past the 18, he pulled up.

Now! Jared forced himself to focus. He could hear a Laser's footsteps charging toward him.

BOOM! Jared swung his leg back and booted the ball. It drove into the back of the net.

Yes! Jared raised his fist in the air. The air filled with shouts and cheers.

"Way to go, Jared!" Ivan called out.

"Goal! Goal!" the Thunder parents yelled.

The play began again. Jared watched for his next chance. Again and again, he drove the ball down the field. He worked the ball through the Laser defense. His teammates called for a pass.

"See me!" Marcus called.

"Wide! Wide!" Ivan yelled from the left sideline.

But Jared swept through the Laser fullbacks by himself. He took shot after shot on goal. Two more times, the ball found the back of the net. Jared jogged to his place after each score. Triumphantly, he looked around at his teammates' faces.

Was it his imagination? Or were his teammates not yelling as they usually did after a score? Jared shrugged.

TWEEEET! The final whistle blew. The Thunder lined up for the final hand slapping with the Lasers.

"You really shut us down," one of the Lasers said to him. Jared felt a little flush of pride run through him.

Jared and his teammates sat on the grass. Coach was finishing his post-game talk. "You defended well today, Thunder. The Lasers didn't score at all."

And we did! Jared wanted to yell out. *I* did! But he kept quiet.

Coach went on. "This will help us against the Hurricane on Thursday. The Hurricane is the last team we have to beat. Then we'll be in the play-offs. Get plenty of rest."

He dismissed the team. Guys got up off the grass. Jared shoved his shoes into his bag. He looked around for Marcus. Marcus was talking with Ivan.

"Hey," Jared called to Marcus.

Marcus looked up. A frown crossed his face. He walked over to Jared.

"I don't know what you're trying to do," he said, looking down at Jared. He shook his head. "You're no ball hog," he said. "Show some respect for your team." Then he turned away.

Jared felt his blood boiling. Everyone wanted him to score. Then when he did, people got mad at him. What was *that* all about?

"Crowley?" Coach's voice called to him.

Jared dragged himself up off the grass. Now was Coach was going to be all over him too?

Coach folded his arms, his clipboard against his chest. "That was the most selfish display I've seen in a long time," he said. "I don't know what's gotten into you, Jared. But whatever it is, try to get rid of it, will you? I need the old Jared back. Your team needs you back. Think about it." He walked away, shaking his head.

Jared clenched his fists. His forehead pounded. This was so unfair. No one understood. He trudged through the parking lot, trying not to hear his teammates talking with one another.

Dad had the car engine running when Jared opened the door. Joad the Toad was in the front seat. Great, he thought. She'd watched the whole game. Dad would be bad enough. He didn't need JoDee adding to it.

"Nice game," JoDee said with a smirk. She turned around and made a face at him. "So," she went on, "this little piggy went to the soccer game. This little piggy scored. How does it feel to be a ball hog?" she asked, laughing.

"Shut up, you toad," Jared barked.

"Jared, be quiet," Dad growled. "And, JoDee, you keep quiet too." He pulled out of the space.

"Oink! Oink!" JoDee hooted.

"JoDee! That's enough!" Dad said sternly. He looked at Jared in the rearview mirror. "I'm not going to say anything to you about your game," he said. "I'm sure you know how I feel."

The car was dead silent all the way home. Once, JoDee snorted from the front seat. Dad glared at her. Jared cracked his knuckles. He wanted to pop her one.

He didn't even want to think about school on Monday. He'd see everyone on the team. Did everyone feel like Marcus did? He winced. Yeah, they probably did. He'd have to fix that. But how? Coach wouldn't let him play in the next game against the Hurricanes. And then no play-off game—and no ODP.

Jared wanted to groan aloud. There was another problem with Monday too. His social studies report was due. That was the last thing he felt like working on.

For the first time in his life, he just wanted to forget about soccer.

10

Game Day

"And that's how we do the Olympics today," Jared said. Standing at the front of the room, he looked around at his classmates. They looked as if they'd been listening. He sighed with relief. Walking over to Mr. Wilson, Jared handed him his notes. Then he dropped down into his seat.

"Well," Mr. Wilson said. He tapped his pencil on the desk. "Not bad information about today's Olympics," he said. "Especially the soccer."

Jared held back a grin. Maybe his grade and the San Diego trip were safe after all. He'd show everyone.

"But," Mr. Wilson continued, "you should have talked more about Greece and the history of the Olympics. *That* was the point of the assignment." He shook his head.

Mr. Wilson looked through the papers Jared had handed him. "Where is your bibliography, Mr. Crowley?" he asked. "I don't see it here."

Bibliography? Jared's heart sank. "Uh, it's not in there?" he asked weakly. "I thought it was . . ." His voice trailed off.

Maribel turned around. Her face looked worried. Jared just shrugged and shook his head. A look of disappointment crossed her face. Jared slumped down in his desk.

"You're the only student not to hand in a bibliography," Mr. Crowley said. "Even our newest student, José, handed one in."

Jared thought the top of his head was going to blow right off. When was he going to shake off José? he wondered. Maybe in Thursday's game, he told himself. Maybe the Hurricane would take out José. Then Coach would have to let Jared play, since he'd scored in the Laser game. Wouldn't he?

At dinner, JoDee smirked across the table at him. "How was your report for Mr. Wilson today?" she asked.

Jared wanted to kick her under the table. Mom and Dad stopped eating.

"Fine," Jared said.

"What was your grade?" asked Dad.

"Uh, I don't know," Jared lied. Here it came, he groaned inwardly.

"He does too know," Joad the Toad exclaimed. A wicked grin spread across her face. "We all got our grades today. Jared just doesn't want to say." She tossed her ponytail.

"Jared?" Mom asked sternly. She waited, her fork in the air.

"Uh, it was a D," Jared admitted. "I just didn't want to ruin dinner by telling you yet."

"That's worth a grounding," Dad said. "You need to be straight with us, Jared."

"That's also no soccer trip to San Diego," Mom added.

Dad sighed. "What's it going to take for you to shape up?"

Jared didn't answer. Why did *he* have to shape up? Why couldn't everyone else see that this wasn't his problem? It was Mr. Wilson who'd given him the bad grade. And it was José who was taking his place on the soccer team. Why couldn't everyone else shape up and leave *him* alone?

The week dragged by until Thursday. Jared saw his teammates at school. He sat with them at lunch and joked around in the hallways. They seemed to be okay, Jared tried to reassure himself. No one mentioned the Laser game or his ball hogging.

Thursday afternoon finally arrived. Hopes high, Jared jogged to join his teammates. Most of them were already warming up on the field. Maybe Coach would play him today. After all, he'd proven he could score again.

The team finished their warm-up drills.

"Come on in," Coach called. Jared joined the cluster of players around Coach.

"This is the game that will send us to the play-offs," Coach said. "The Sting has lost only to us. We lost our only game to them. We need to beat the Hurricane." He looked around at the players. "Focus and do your best."

He called out the starters. Jared listened for his name, but Coach didn't call it. With a sigh, he stood on the sideline and watched the game begin.

What if something happened to José? Maybe then Coach would put him in. Jared shifted uncomfortably. He felt guilty even thinking like that. But if it was the only way to get to the play-offs and the ODP . . .

The Hurricane team won the toss, and play began. Finding a hole in the Thunder defense, the Hurricane offense began working the ball down the field. They passed crisply, the ball moving through the Thunder fullbacks. What was going on? Jared wanted to yell out. Where was the defense?

Suddenly Chas snagged a pass in midfield. He wheeled and sent a hard pass upfield to KeShaun. KeShaun dodged a Hurricane midfielder. He sent a blistering pass past the half line to José.

Just as José trapped the ball with his thigh, a Hurricane midfielder slid into him.

Thud! José hit the turf hard. The ball squirted out to the right.

"Red card!" the Thunder crowd yelled.

"All ball, ref! All ball!" the Hurricane crowd yelled.

The ref held his arms up. "Play on!" he yelled.

But for once, José didn't scramble to his feet. He rolled on the ground, his leg twisted under him. Jared stared in disbelief. José was down! Was this his chance?

"Player down!" Coach Mulvey hollered. The ref stopped watching the action. He turned and blew the whistle. Coach and Chas helped José hobble off the field.

Now! Jared told himself. His heart leaped. Coach *had* to put him in. Then he'd score and lead the Thunder into the play-offs.

He held his breath.

"Crowley?" Coach yelled. He motioned to Jared. Heart pumping, Jared jogged into the game. He turned to show his jersey number to the ref.

TWEEEET! The ref began play again.

The Hurricane defense looked like a sea of yellow shirts to Jared. He stormed through the midfield desperately looking for open space. There! He turned at the 18 and watched Ivan work the ball downfield.

"Ivan!" Jared yelled. He crouched on the balls of his feet, ready for the pass.

Ivan hesitated for a second. Then he sent a hard cross to Jared.

Jared's hands felt clammy. He had to score!

He trapped the ball with his chest and settled it with his heel. Behind him, he could hear the pounding feet of a Hurricane player.

"Man on!" Kevin yelled to him.

BOOM! Jared booted the ball toward the far post. Please! Please! he begged silently.

The crowd groaned as the ball zoomed wide of the goal. Ivan had waited too long to pass to him, Jared grumbled to himself. Ivan should have crossed it sooner. Then the Hurricane defender wouldn't have forced Jared to take his shot too early.

Disappointed, Jared jockeyed for position again. The Hurricane keeper flung the ball hard over the players' heads.

Jared watched Marcus speed past the last defender. Marcus trapped the ball with his thigh. He looked around.

See me! Jared wanted to yell. He was open! Just then, the Hurricane sweeper challenged Jared. Marcus knocked the ball toward the right sideline. Slicing in from behind Marcus, Kevin snagged it.

Kevin slipped through the Hurricane defenders. The ball rolled fast across the wet grass. Then Kevin kicked the ball hard. The scorching shot cannoned toward the far post.

"Goal! Goal!" the crowd yelled. The Hurricane keeper dove for it. But the ball found its mark.

Jared hung his head. It looked as if he wasn't going to get another pass from anyone. He'd have to be a ball hog again, no matter what.

Three more times, Jared shoved his way through the defense to the ball. He cradled it between his feet, racing down the field. Plunging through the yellow shirts, he took the shots.

Every shot missed. He could hear his teammates yelling.

"Cross!"

"Pass! See the player!"

But Jared gritted his teeth. No one would pass to him, so he had to score by himself. It wasn't his fault.

With 20 minutes left, the score was Thunder–1, Hurricane–0. The Hurricane defenders began playing more aggressively. They marked the Thunder offense, shadowing their every move.

Jared struggled to avoid them. He snatched the ball from between the feet of a Hurricane midfielder. Turning, he began working the ball downfield.

"See me!" Roy yelled from the 18.

No chance, Jared told himself. He had to do this himself.

He twisted past the yellow-shirted sweeper. He reached the top of the box, the ball safely at his feet. Now! he told himself.

SMACK! He sidefooted the ball in a sharp chip. Hopes high, he watched it arc up toward the corner of the net.

The Hurricane keeper jumped up. He punched the ball away. It bounced out-of-bounds.

Jared almost groaned aloud. He'd missed again.

"Sub!" Coach Mulvey yelled.

With a sinking heart, Jared heard his name.

"Crowley? Come on out," Coach called.

Jared jogged off the field. He wanted to hold his head high. But he couldn't help seeing his teammates looking away.

Coming on to the field, Jon high-fived him. "Nice tries," Jon said.

Jared flung himself onto the grass next to the other subs. José sat a few yards away. His ankle was covered with an ice bag.

In a daze, Jared watched the last minutes of the game. What was he going to do now? He'd blown his chance to score. The play-off game would go on without him—and most likely the Olympic Development Program as well.

He grimaced, remembering Joad the Toad's taunt. "Mr. Magic . . . the soccer stud . . . can't be bothered to practice." Jared sighed and closed his eyes.

Maybe he *was* too much of a hotshot. Maybe Coach and his parents—and everyone else—was right. Maybe playing at this level did mean he had to work harder. Maybe it wasn't everyone else's fault, but his own.

Jared almost winced. In his head, he could see the shots on goal he used to make. They'd arced through the air and found the magnet at the back of the net.

But the magnet was gone now. It had disappeared when he'd stopped practicing and working with his teammates. He had to wake up, he admitted to himself. If he wanted to play for the ODP, he had to make some changes. Jared groaned silently. It would take a lot of work to catch up.

"Hey," a voice said. Jared looked up. José had hobbled over to him.

Not *now*! Jared felt his forehead beginning to pound. Couldn't José see that he wanted to be left alone?

José dropped down next to Jared with a grunt. He flinched, adjusting his ankle and the ice pack.

"You want to take shots with me sometime this week?" José asked. Jared narrowed his eyes. What was José up to now? Or was he really being nice? The guy looked sincere, Jared decided finally.

José went on. "I—uh—on my other team in San Carlos," he began, "I kind of took it for granted that I could always shoot. I stopped working so hard. Then a new guy came on the team and took my position. I had to practice all the time just to get it back."

Jared stared at José in disbelief.

"So," José finished, "I've been there too."

Jared's jaw dropped. José had once had scoring problems? But he never missed!

"That's why I work so hard," José continued. "Maybe we could work hard together," he offered, shrugging his shoulders. "It helps to work with another striker."

Why not? Jared asked himself. He had nothing to lose. Things couldn't get any worse, could they?

"Ah, sure," Jared said.

José grinned. "We'll take care of all of them," he said. "*Trabajemos como burros!*"

"*Sí*," Jared said, grinning. "*Como burros!*"

TWEEEET! The game ended— Hurricane–1, Thunder–2.

The Thunder crowd cheered. The players jumped on one another, hooting and yelling.

"The play-offs!" Marcus yelled. "We're going to the play-offs!"

Yes, they were, Jared repeated silently. And he would be a part of it. With a lot of hard work and practice, he'd make sure of it.